The Three Swingin' Pigs

Vicky Rubin

Illustrated by Rhode Montijo

HENRY HOLT AND COMPANY · NEW YORK

Henry Holt and Company, LLC, *Publishers since 1866*
175 Fifth Avenue, New York, New York 10010
www.henryholtchildrensbooks.com

Henry Holt® is a registered trademark of Henry Holt and Company, LLC.
Text copyright © 2007 by Vicky Rubin. Illustrations copyright © 2007 by Rhode Montijo.
All rights reserved. Distributed in Canada by H. B. Fenn and Company Ltd.

Library of Congress Cataloging-in-Publication Data
Rubin, Vicky.
The three swingin' pigs / Vicky Rubin; illustrated by Rhode Montijo.—1st ed.
p.   cm.
Summary: This version of the traditional English tale depicts three musical pigs
who try to win Wolfie over with their vivacious vocals and toe-tapping tunes.
ISBN-13: 978-0-8050-7335-5 / ISBN-10: 0-8050-7335-3
[1. Pigs—Folklore. 2. Wolves—Folklore. 3. Folklore—England.]
I. Montijo, Rhode, ill. II. Three little pigs. III. Title. IV. Title: Three swinging pigs.
PZ8.R8157Th 2006   398.2—dc22   [E]   2006002870

First Edition—2007 / Designed by Laurent Linn
The artist used acrylic paint on canvas to create the illustrations for this book.
Printed in the United States of America on acid-free paper. ∞

1 3 5 7 9 10 8 6 4 2

To my Daddy-O, "Doc" Rubin, who knows how to keep a beat
—V. R.

For Pam Howe, Jamie Baker, Dave Gordon, and Reka Simonsen,
who all helped make the dream a reality
—R. M.

Once and only once there were three pigs who kept perfect rhythm.

Satch played sax. *Wee-wee-wee-wee!*

Mo played bass. *Doont-doont—dun-duhhh!*

And Ella sang. *Scat-scooby-dooby, scat-scooby-dooby, skit-scat-skedoodle, shoooo!*

The Three Swingin' Pigs performed in roadside dives no bigger than a trough and dance halls huge enough to hold a herd of cattle. And wherever they played, audiences went wild.

But in the Hogland Woods there lived a wolf, and he was *baaaaaad*. On a typical wolf day, he ate up six coach mice, sat down on other people's tuffets, and went around in the most unwolflike of getups.

"What did you expect?" he said. "I'm a classic fairy-tale villain."

The wolf was not only the baddest cat to
walk the land, he had the baddest breath in
the land. It's no wonder that he didn't have
any friends.

One day, the wolf heard music on the radio. *"Skit-scat-skedoodle, shoooo!"* The pigs! He had to admit the tune was catchy. His toes tapped. His claws snapped. He sang along. He couldn't help it! "STOP," he barked. "I remember what their uncles did to me, just because I sneezed on their bungalows. I let them get away, but these three won't."

"That was the Three Swingin' Pigs with their latest hit. Don't miss the hottest jazz trio ever to hit Hooland, tonight at

"At last," said the wolf. "Now I can DEVOUR the Three Swingin' Pigs—with barbecue sauce—in front of a live audience. Littlepiggie Hall, here I come!"

The wolf went to buy a ticket.

"Sorry, furry fellow, we're *allll* sold out."

"But I've got to eat those pigs—I mean, meet those pigs. I'm their biggest fan!"

"Don't be a square, Daddy-O. Don't be uptight. When I get like that I take a deep breath and count to ten—that's right—ahhhh."

"Ahhhh," said the wolf. "How soooothing. Aha! There's the Pigmobile! Feet, don't fail me now!"

'Round midnight he caught up to the pigs as they sipped a cup of java—that's coffee, black. He was about to pounce when he heard Satch say, "Tomorrow is the Big Pig Gig at the Smokehouse! We'll play so loud we'll blow the house down. I mean, they'll love us," he added quickly. "Say, what's that smell?"

"Perfect!" said the wolf. "I will swallow them in one gulp in front of all of Hogland. Soon those silly swinging swine will be hoofnotes in musical history!"

The next night, the ticket line at the Smokehouse
stretched all the way to the forest! "Stupid pig
fans," the wolf snorted. "Ridiculous. No, I don't
want any souvenirs!"

Finally he reached the window. "Front-row seat."

"Sorry, sir. All I've got is one back in the hallway,
near the rest rooms."

"Oh, for goodness—all right."

The aisles were filled with fans tapping their toes, snapping their claws, and singing along with the Three Swingin' Pigs. The wolf elbowed his way forward, using his bad breath to clear the way. At last he got to the front.

Satch was playing sax. *Wee-wee-wee-wee!*

Mo was playing bass. *Doont-doont—dun-duhhh!*

And Ella was singing. *"Scat-scooby-dooby, scat-scooby-dooby, skit-skat-skedoodle, shoooo!"*

The wolf felt his toes starting to tap and his claws starting to snap. He heard himself singing along. "STOP!" he barked.

"Did you hear that?" said Satch.

"I smell it! It's the wolf!" said Mo. "Our uncles warned us this could happen!"

"Don't flip your lid, don't snap your cap, just stay cool, boys," Ella cooed. "Music soothes the stinky beast."

"Hope you're right," said Satch and Mo.

"Now, I'm going to sing a song," Ella called out, "and when I sing, everybody sing after me! But first, how about a volunteer up here? You, sir, in the natty suit."

"Me?" said the wolf. Was she crazy?

"Yes you, Daddy-O. What's your name?"

"W–Wolfie," said the wolf, trembling. All those eyes were staring at him! "Uh, B-Big, B-Baad Wolfie."

"You know, our uncles met you way back when. What was it that you said to them?"

"I said I'd huff and I'd puff and I'd blow the house down."

Ella called out, "Sing it! *He'll HUFF and he'll PUFF and he'll blow the house DOWN!*"

The audience sang, "*He'll HUFF and he'll PUFF and he'll blow the house DOWN!*"

"Sing it, Wolfie!" said Ella.

"*I'll HUFF and I'll PUFF and I'll blow the house DOWN!*" he squeaked.

"Let's hear it for Wolfie!" Ella called.
The audience mooed and brayed. It stamped
and snorted. "YEAH, WOLFIE!"
"Now let's see you huff and puff!" she said.
Wolfie took a deep breath.
Ella sang, "Scooby doo wah, scooby doo woah,
Satch, please help this ol' wolf blow!"
Satch put his sax into the wolf's open choppers.
BWWWEEEEEEAAAAHHHHHHH! played Wolfie.
The crowd practically stampeded. "Hurrah! "

No one had ever cheered for Wolfie before. In fact, no one had ever LIKED him before. He was enjoying this!

But wait! He still had to eat the pigs. "Farewell, my little hambones!"

"Wolfie," said Ella. "Wouldn't you rather make music, sweet music, than eat three perspiring pigs?"

"But I'm supposed to—" said Wolfie. "Though I also want—let me take a time out." He took a deep breath.

"AAAAAHHHHHHH. YES! If I eat you pudgy porkers, I won't be able to howl with the band. And at last I've found what I REALLY love. It's music. Sweet music." And he howled. "AWOOOOOOOOOOOOO!"

"Have a cool peppermint for that wolf breath," said Mo.

"Thanks," said Wolfie.

Ella called out, "Ladies and gentlemen, meet our newest member, Wolfie, the Biggest, Baaaaaadest, Howlin' Wolf in the land!"

And EVERYBODY sang.

"Skit-scat-skedaddle, skit-scat-skedaddle, skit-scat-skedoodle, aWOOOOOOOO!"

356740-16725421